For the city of Elkader

With special thanks to Bonnie Geisert, Trisha Finley, and David and Lisa Pope
for their help and encouragement on this project.

All of the illustrations in this book were produced from copperplate etchings
that were first hand printed and then hand colored using watercolor.

www.enchantedlion.com

First Edition published in 2018 by Enchanted Lion Books,
67 West Street, 317A, Brooklyn, New York 11222
Text and illustration copyright © 2018 by Arthur Geisert
Production and layout: Marc Drumwright
All rights reserved under International and Pan-American Copyright Conventions.
A CIP record is on file with the Library of Congress
ISBN: 978-1-59270-265-7
1 3 5 7 9 8 6 4 2

Printed in China by RR Donnelley Asia Printing Solutions Ltd.
First Printing

Pumpkin Island

Arthur Geisert

ENCHANTED LION BOOKS

NEW YORK

A storm approached a small farmstead at the edge of town. There was just enough time to get inside before it rained, hard and long.

The river rose out of its banks and swept a pumpkin downstream.

The pumpkin broke into pieces when it hit a small island. The soil there was very rich, so before long, the pumpkin's seeds began to sprout. Vines grew and stretched across the river, all the way to the bridge.

The vines grew and grew.

Soon pumpkins began to appear.

Then they began popping up all over town.

People did fun things with the pumpkins.

Sometimes, even dangerous things.

They built catapults.

And held contests to see who could fling a pumpkin the farthest.

Some of the townspeople decided to decorate.

When Main Street was all filled up with pumpkins, the town held its very first pumpkin festival.

People made pumpkin bread and pumpkin pie, and sweet pumpkin spice to serve with their coffee.

Eventually, the pumpkin vines made their way into the alleys, where giant pumpkins ripened in the sun.

These were collected, cut in half, and turned into other things.

Like boats and little houses.

The pumpkins were everywhere!

And they just kept growing.

They became such a problem that people started carting them away to the abandoned stone quarry.

Fortunately, it was almost Halloween.

The townspeople collected hundreds of pumpkins and carved them into jack-o'-lanterns.

The pumpkins were lit and the town held its biggest Halloween celebration ever.

Jack-o'-lanterns glowed from the rooftops and through the streets and alleys.

People celebrated long and late into the night.

Afterwards, all the vines were cut and the pumpkins were turned into mulch, which was spread throughout the town.

The following spring, the flowers were more beautiful than ever.